MARGRET & H.A. REY'S
Curious George
Goes to a Costume Party

Illustrated in the style of H. A. Rey by Martha Weston

Houghton Mifflin Company   Boston 2001

Library of Congress Cataloging-in-Publication Data

Curious George goes to a costume party / illustrated in the style of H. A. Rey by Martha Weston.
p.   cm.
Based on the original character by Margret and H. A. Rey.
Summary: Curious George inadvertently causes a sensation at his first Halloween costume party.
RNF ISBN 0-618-06564-4   PAP ISBN 0-618-06569-5
[1. Monkeys—Fiction. 2. Halloween—Fiction. 3. Parties—Fiction. 4. Humorous stories.]
I. Title: Margret and H. A. Rey's Curious George goes to a costume party. II. Title: Curious
George goes to a costume party. III. Rey, Margret, 1906–1996. IV. Rey, H. A. (Hans Augusto),
1898–1977 V. Weston, Martha. VI. Title.
PZ7.M335855   2000
[E]—dc21

This is George.

He was a good little monkey and always very curious.

One day George and his friend, the man with the yellow hat, were on their way to a party at Mrs. Gray's house.

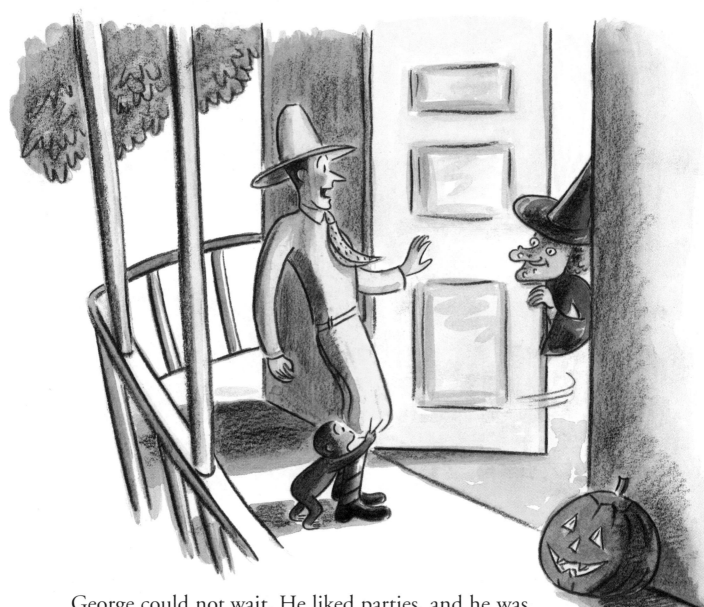

George could not wait. He liked parties, and he was looking forward to seeing Mrs. Gray. But when the door opened George did not see Mrs. Gray at all—he saw a witch!

"Don't be afraid, George," said the man with the yellow hat. "This witch is our friend."

The witch took off her mask. It was Mrs. Gray after all! "Oh dear," she said, "did I forget to tell you this was a costume party?"

George had never been to a costume party before. Inside he saw more people that he knew. They were all wearing costumes. There was his friend Betsy dressed up like an astronaut. And was that Bill? Why, he looked just like a mummy!

6

George wanted to wear a costume, too.
"I have some dress-up clothes upstairs,"
said Mrs. Gray. "Would you like to
use them to make a costume, George?"

Mrs. Gray took George to
a room with a big trunk filled
with clothes.

"Borrow anything you like,
George," she said. "I have
just the thing for your friend
downstairs."

George tried on lots of costumes.

The first was too big.

The next was too small.

Another was too silly.

And this one was too scary!

At last George found a costume that was just right. George was a rodeo cowboy! He wore a vest and pants with fringe. He even had a lasso and a hat!

10

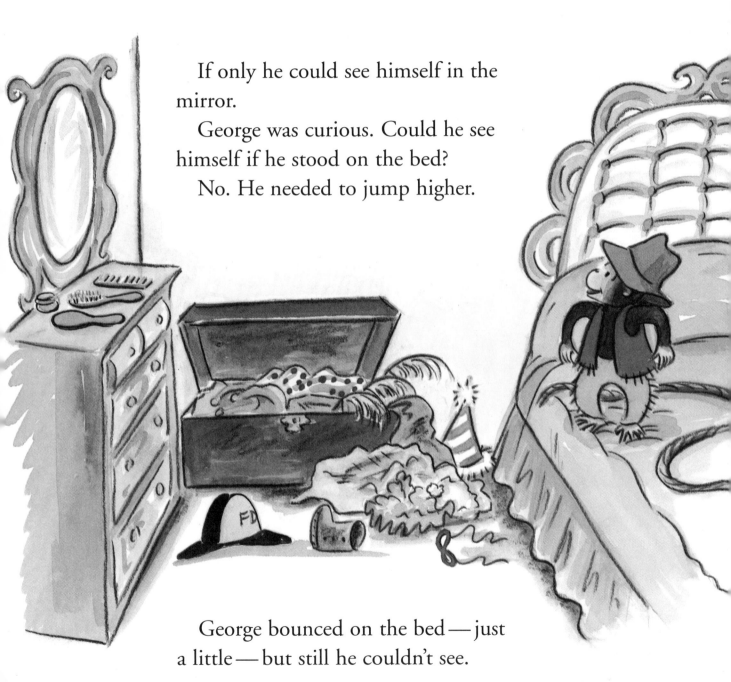

If only he could see himself in the mirror.

George was curious. Could he see himself if he stood on the bed?

No. He needed to jump higher.

George bounced on the bed — just a little — but still he couldn't see.

He bounced a little more, and a little more.

Soon George was having so much fun he forgot all about looking in the mirror. He bounced as high as he could until—

CRASH!—George bounced off the bed. He smashed into the night table and got tangled up in the tablecloth. Suddenly everything went dark.

George heard the people downstairs gasp, "What was that?"

"Was that a ghost?"

14

A ghost?! George did not want to meet up with a ghost alone. He dashed out of the room and down the hall. He wanted to get back to his friend in a hurry and he knew the fastest way.

He hopped onto the
stair rail and sailed —
WHOOSH! — down
the stairs.

"It *is* a ghost!" someone screamed. Everyone turned. They looked scared, and they were looking at George. The ghost must be right behind him!

George flew off the rail and landed — PLOP! — in the arms of a farmer. But this wasn't really a farmer. It was his friend, the man with the yellow hat!

Soon everyone stopped looking scared and started to laugh.

"That's not a ghost. That's a cowboy!" laughed a policeman.
"That's not a cowboy. That's a monkey!" giggled a princess.
"That's not just any monkey," said Betsy. "It's Curious George!"
Everyone clapped and cheered. They liked George's Halloween trick.

"You gave us a good scare, George," said Mrs. Gray. "And I'm glad to see you found some interesting costumes. Now why don't I take your ghost outfit so you can join the party?"

After the guests bobbed for apples, lit jack-o'-lanterns, and played some party games, prizes for the best costumes were handed out.

There was one prize for Betsy, and one
for Bill, and *two* for Curious George.

"You were the best ghost *and* the best
cowboy, George," said Mrs. Gray.

Everyone had a good time at the party, especially George.
Too soon it was time to say goodbye.

"Good night, George."
Happy Halloween!